DREAMWORKS

KUNG FU PANDA
LEGENDS OF AWESOMENESS
nickelodeon.

Long Live the Dragon Warrior

adapted by Tracey West

Simon Spotlight
New York London Toronto Sydney New Delhi

SIMON SPOTLIGHT
An imprint of Simon & Schuster Children's Publishing Division
1230 Avenue of the Americas, New York, New York 10020
This Simon Spotlight edition June 2015
© 2015 Viacom International Inc. All Rights Reserved. NICKELODEON and all related logos are trademarks of Viacom International Inc. Based on the feature film "Kung Fu Panda," © 2008 DreamWorks Animation LLC. All Rights Reserved. All rights reserved, including the right of reproduction in whole or in part in any form. SIMON SPOTLIGHT and colophon are registered trademarks of Simon & Schuster, Inc. For information about special discounts for bulk purchases, please contact Simon & Schuster Special Sales at 1-866-506-1949 or business@simonandschuster.com.
Designed by Bob Steimle
Manufactured in the United States of America 0515 OFF
10 9 8 7 6 5 4 3 2 1
ISBN 978-1-4814-2749-4 (pbk)
ISBN 978-1-4814-2750-0 (hc)
ISBN 978-1-4814-2751-7 (eBook)

CHALLENGE DAY

CHAPTER ONE

"O nly by achieving inner peace can a true kung-fu master unfold like a lotus flower," Master Shifu said in a calming voice.

Tigress, Viper, Mantis, Monkey, and Crane posed in a circle around

him, their eyes closed in deep meditation. It was part of the Furious Five's daily training.

The sound of Po's voice interrupted the peaceful silence.

"*Aaaaaaaah!* Is that all you got? It's gonna take

more than that to defeat the Dragon Warrior!"

Master Shifu and the Furious Five burst out of the Jade Palace, ready to help defend Po. Who was attacking him? A powerful warrior? An army of ninjas?

"Come on, you," Po whined, trying to stretch a hammock between bamboo poles. "I just want to take a nap!"

Then he looked up and saw the others. "Oh, hey, guys. How goes the meditating?"

"It was fine until we rushed to save you from your 'attacker,'" Mantis replied.

"Yeah, sweet hammock, huh?" Po said, sitting in it. It pulled back like a slingshot and catapulted him across the courtyard, causing him to knock down the Furious Five on his way!

Tigress jumped to her feet, her eyes blazing. "Master Shifu, can we head into the Training Hall? Suddenly I'm in the mood to hit something."

Shifu nodded and then turned to Po. "Will you be joining us?"

"Um . . . I kinda pulled my gluttonous maximus

wrestling with the hammock here, so I think I'll just chill a little," Po replied, settling in for a nap.

Master Shifu shook his head. Po had forgotten what it meant to be the Dragon Warrior. Shifu had to find a way to make him remember.

Suddenly, he had an idea. . . .

The next morning, Shifu gathered Po and the Furious Five together.

"You've all been working very hard and deserve a day of relaxation," he told them. "I'm sending you to the Xiu Xhan Hot Springs."

"Yes!" cried Po as he followed the others.

But Master Shifu stopped him. "You're staying here."

Po frowned. "I really need a break. I was dreaming all night that I was awake, and it was exhausting."

"I have urgent Dragon Warrior business for you to handle," said Shifu. "I need you to go to the village and get me . . . an apple."

"An apple?" asked Po.

"An apple," said Shifu.

"An apple?" Po asked again.

"An apple," Shifu replied.

"Seriously?" Po asked. "'Cause I could do more than that."

"I know," said Shifu. "Just an apple will do."

Po had no idea why an apple was so important. But he made his way down to the village just the same.

He stopped in front of the first apple cart he saw. He was trying to decide which apple to choose when he saw a small pig staring up at him. Then, suddenly . . .

"Aaaaiiieeeeee!"

The pig leaped up and attacked Po!

CHAPTER **TWO**

The pig knocked down Po, and Po's foot got stuck in a bucket. But once Po was back up, the pig was no match for the Dragon Warrior. Po scooped up the little guy with one paw.

"Had a bad day?" Po asked, and put down the pig.

Then Po turned back to the apple stand and reached for an apple.

Muh Lin, the goose running the stand, slapped his paw. Po reached again, and Muh Lin slapped him again. Then Muh Lin dove across the apples, knocking Po on his back.

Po stood up, and turned to see a group of villagers behind him, staring in his direction. They all looked ready to fight.

"Something weird is going on here," Po realized. He quickly ran out of the village—and right into Master Shifu and Zeng, the palace messenger.

"I'm still waiting for my apple, panda," Master Shifu said.

"Master Shifu!" Po cried, relieved. "I'm having that nightmare where everyone attacks me while I'm naked."

"Po, you're wearing pants," Shifu pointed out. "And besides, you're awake. Anyway, I forgot to tell you. Today is Dragon Warrior Challenge Day. On the hundredth day of being Dragon Warrior, anyone can challenge you. If you're defeated before sunset, the victor takes your title."

"What? I could lose my Dragon Warriorshipdom? That's terrible!" Po cried.

"You're not up to the challenge?" Shifu asked.

"Uh, sure I am," Po replied. He launched into a series of kung-fu kicks and spins. "Bring it!" he cried, and he ran back into the village.

Zeng looked at Shifu. "But, sir, it's a lie," said the gray goose. "There is no Dragon Warrior Challenge Day."

"It's a lesson," Shifu said. "This is just the thing to make Po take being Dragon Warrior seriously. And with the Furious Five gone, there is no one in

the village strong enough to beat him."

Master Shifu was right. There was no one *inside* the village strong enough to beat Po. But there was one *outside* the village.

Hundun the rhino had faced Po before—and lost his horn. He spent his days in Chor-Ghom prison, carving new horns in his cell and attaching them to what was left of his broken one. That's where he was when one of the guards told him about Dragon Warrior Challenge Day.

"Too bad you're locked up in here instead of out there fighting your sworn enemy," the guard taunted him.

"Yes. Too bad," Hundun replied. "Care to look at my latest horn? I just finished it."

He slipped the horn through the bars of his cell and stepped back.

Boom! The horn exploded, knocking the prison guard off his feet and blasting away the cell bars. Hundun stepped out into freedom.

"I will crush the Dragon Warrior and pluck his title, like I pluck a yam from a tree and squeeze its squishiness, the way one would squeeze a squishy yam of revenge!" he roared with an evil laugh. "Ready or not, Po. Here I come!"

CHAPTER THREE

Back in the village, Po was busy defending his title. Every duck, goat, rabbit, and pig wanted their chance to become the Dragon Warrior. Mrs. Yoon, a sweet, elderly goat, whacked Po with her cane. Even his own father tried to take him down with a wok!

That's how it went all day. Po jumped from rooftop to rooftop as villagers chased him with rakes and pitchforks. One by one, he fought them off.

Fang, a young rabbit who idolized Po, even wanted to take a shot. He jumped on a chimney.

"Time for . . . ," he shouted, and then the chimney cracked underneath him.

"Aaaaaaaaaaah!"

Po looked up and caught the falling bunny just in time. Then he protected Fang's body with his own as the heavy stone chimney tipped and began to fall toward them.

"This is gonna sting," Po said, cringing.

Boom! The stone landed on Po. Fang was okay and quickly hopped away. But Po had hurt his left leg.

"Everybody okay?" he asked in a daze as he tried to stand. Then he fell flat on his face. He had taken a big hit!

"No more fighting," announced Mr. Liu, a goat. "You saved Fang and proved once again the reason why you are our Dragon Warrior."

"You mean *was* your Dragon Warrior!" some-
one with a deep voice thundered behind Po.

Po turned around to see Hundun standing
there.

Pow! The rhino hit him with a powerful punch that sent him sprawling.

"You didn't think I'd miss out on a chance like Challenge Day, did you?" Hundun asked.

Pow! He punched Po again.

Po slowly stood up, trying to not put pressure on his hurt leg. "Hundun, do you really want to say you only beat me 'cause I'm hurt and exhausted?"

"I'm good with that," Hundun replied.

Pow! Another punch sent Po flying.

Bam! Hundun followed up with a kick.

Po tried to sit up, but he was dizzy.

Pow! The next punch knocked Po out cold. Hundun triumphantly put his massive foot on Po's chest.

"All hail me!" he thundered. "The new Dragon Warrior of the Valley of Peace's Dragon Warrior!"

CHAPTER **FOUR**

Hundun stomped up to the Jade Palace.

"Bow to your new Dragon Warrior!" he announced. Master Shifu and Zeng were stunned.

"You defeated Po?" Master Shifu asked.

Hundun merely growled in reply.

"No matter," said Shifu. "There is no Challenge Day. I made it up. You are no more Dragon Warrior than Zeng there."

"What?" Hundun cried.

Hundun smacked his hands against his head. "Stupid, stupid, stupid! Why do I keep thinking good things can happen to me? A stupid rhino with no horn."

Then his eyes lit up. "Wait a minute. If no one else knows that you made it up, and they don't find out, then the lie will actually work as truthfully as if it were actually the truthful truth! If everyone believes I'm the Dragon Warrior, then you're the only one who can tell them different."

He tried to kick Shifu, but the kung-fu master expertly dodged and jumped up to hit Hundun's face. Then he jumped down and spun his cane like a weapon. Hundun grabbed one end of the cane, struggling to control it.

"You'll have to do better than that, Hundun," Shifu said.

"Fine! How about this?" Hundun asked.

The top of his fake horn flipped open. Three arrows flew out and struck Master Shifu. The poison in the arrows knocked him out cold. Hundun tossed Shifu into a wood box. Zeng was so frightened, he climbed into the box himself and shut the door.

"I am the Dragon Warrior!" Hundun roared.

Then he stomped down to the village. He smashed the musicians' instruments. He demanded free apples from Muh Lin. He stole Mrs. Yoon's basket of steamed buns.

"This is *my* village now!" he announced, stuffing his mouth with stolen food.

Over at the noodle shop, Po was recovering with the help of his dad. Mr. Ping looked out

37

his window and saw Hundun bullying everyone.

"Po, Hundun is wrecking our village! Help them!" he pleaded.

"What am I gonna do, Dad? Huh? He's the Dragon Warrior now," Po said, defeated.

Then little Fang jumped in the window, striking a kung-fu pose.

"*Yaa!* I'm going to defeat the Dragon Warrior!" he announced.

"Uh, hate to break it to you, Fang, but you're a little late," Po said.

"I don't wanna fight you. I wanna fight Hundun, the Dragon Warrior! There's still time. The sun hasn't set," Fang said. Then he quickly hopped away.

A wave of hope filled Po. He picked up his father. "I still have time, Dad! I can still beat Hundun!"

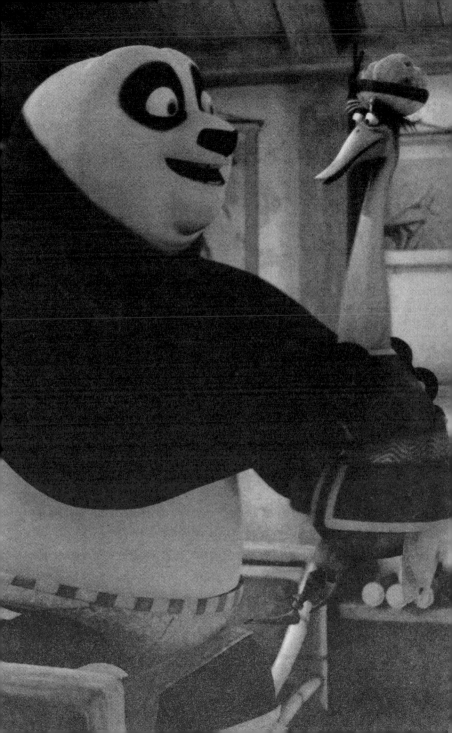

CHAPTER FIVE

Po grabbed a walking stick and made his way outside as quickly as he could. The sun was getting dangerously low in the sky.

He found Hundun holding Fang upside down by one hand. The little rabbit kicked Hundun hard in the nose.

Hundun growled. "After I crush you, I'm gonna crush this whole sorry village!"

Po limped up to him. "You like picking on adorable, furry creatures, Hundun? Well I got your adorable, furry creature right here!"

Whack! Po used the walking stick to take Hundun by surprise. Then he jumped up and used his good leg to deliver a second blow. The big rhino went flying.

Po grinned at his success. He was winning.

"Now maybe you'll think twice before you—whoa!"

Hundun charged at Po. Po grabbed the rhino's head and pushed Hundun away.

"You have no chance, Po! You taught me your kung-fu secrets long ago!" Hundun reminded

him. He broke Po's cane in half. Then he took off his fake horn and replaced it with a sharp sword!

He charged at Po again, this time moving very surely and swiftly. As Po ducked to avoid the sword, Hundun landed blow after blow on Po's face. Then he grabbed Po and hurled him into a stone wall. Po fell facedown.

"Can't ... hold out ... much longer," Po said weakly.

Hundun pressed a foot down on the back of Po's neck. "Perfect. Now you can enjoy your permanent nap of permanence, which is long and without ending. Permanently!"

As Hundun walked away, Po opened his eyes. "This can't be happening," he said, and then it hit him. "And I can't let it happen."

He got to his feet. "I've had enough of this, Hundun. I hope you won't be too sad about not being the Dragon Warrior anymore."

"Too late! The sun has set!" Hundun said, pointing to the sky. "I am and always will be the Dragon Warrior!"

"No!" Po said firmly. "It's not about the title. It's about what's right."

Hundun angrily charged. Po looked around. Then he saw just what he needed: a hammock.

Po jumped on the hammock and propelled himself forward, like a stone coming out of a slingshot. He crashed into Hundun.

"Aaaaah!" The force sent Hundun crashing through a house.

He was down for the count.

The villagers let out a cheer. Po would always be their Dragon Warrior.

And Po would

never forget it. When he got back to the Jade Palace, he freed Master Shifu and Zeng.

"Oh, Po, you succeeded. Thank goodness!" Shifu said.

"No, I failed," Po admitted. "The sun had already

set before I could beat Hundun. I never should have taken being Dragon Warrior for granted. It was a gift I was given, and I ruined it."

"Well, Challenge Day was a teeny-weeny bit made up," Shifu confessed.

"You lied to me?" Po asked. "That's . . . awesome!"

That meant Po was still the Dragon Warrior.

And he would never take it for granted again!

THE KUNG-FU KID

CHAPTER ONE

From then on, Po spent less time napping and more time training.

Of course, that didn't mean that he stopped napping. In fact, one afternoon, Po fell asleep while training with Master Shifu. He was snoring loudly as Shifu tried to play calming music on his flute.

Then Po heard a noise and woke with a start. He grabbed the flute and went into attack mode—but it was only Zeng. He was carrying a crown made of green leaves.

"Your crown for the Peace Jubilee, Dragon Warrior," Zeng said.

Po's face lit up. "The olive-branch crown, for me! Yay!"

He took the crown and put it on. It looked tiny on his giant head.

"Po, this is the Peace Jubilee, not the 'Attack Zeng with a Flute' Jubilee," Shifu reminded him.

"Just trying to stay ready in case Temutai tries to squish my head," Po explained. Temutai was a big, strong water buffalo warrior and king of the Qidan Clan.

"Nonsense," said Shifu. "Hostilities are strictly forbidden during the Peace Jubilee, even with the warriors of the Qidan. They are our guests."

The Furious Five walked into the palace courtyard. Tigress raised her eyebrows when she saw Po.

"Wait, Po's wearing the olive-branch crown?" she asked. "Traditionally, one of the Furious Five leads the ceremony."

"C'mon, Tigress. The jubilee needs some new blood—a fresh face!" Po said. "Plus, I get to wear the crown!"

Tigress grinned. "Po's right."

"I am?" Po asked, surprised.

"Yes. Because it also means he'll have to judge the children's kung-fu matches." She walked away smugly.

Po wasn't sure what Tigress was getting at,

but he was too excited to worry about it. He and Master Shifu went to the top steps of the palace to greet their guests.

"Presenting the Warrior King of the Qidan, Temutai!" announced a water buffalo.

A huge water buffalo three times the size of the first one came up the stairs, huffing and puffing. Temutai had an olive-branch crown perched on top of his horns.

"Thank you for accepting our offering of peace on this day," said Shifu.

Temutai's eyes blazed red. "I have only one thing to say about this so-called Peace Jubilee!" he said. Po's eyes narrowed. Was Temutai looking for trouble?

Then Temutai broke into a grin. "Are these crowns awesome or what?"

"I know, right?" Po agreed.

"Have you tried it at a jaunty angle?" Temutai asked.

Po pointed to the top of his head. "Livin' it!"

They walked down into the village. Po and Temutai took seats on the judging platform. The crowd cheered as Po stood to start the festivities.

"Thank you, citizens!" Po called out. "I now declare this Peace Jubilee open!"

CHAPTER **TWO**

The excited villagers cheered.

"And to start the festivities, the annual children's kung-fu matches!" Po cried.

The villagers groaned.

Po frowned. What was so bad about the children's matches?

He quickly found out.

The kids were well . . . still learning. A pig and

a bunny got into a slap fight. A goat and another bunny accidentally bonked heads together. A tiny goose was too afraid to use his kung fu. Before he knew it, Po was dozing off—and so was Temutai.

Shifu nudged them awake.

"You guys are awesome!" Po said as the young future warriors lined up in front of him, with hopeful smiles on their faces. "It's gonna be real tough to pick a winner."

"Wait," Temutai cried. "I have one more competitor. My little nephew, Jing Mei!"

Thump! Thump! Thump!

The platform shook as the young water buffalo stomped toward them. He towered over the other kids and was as wide as all of them put together.

"Ready, Uncle," he said in a deep voice.

"Your 'little' nephew?" Po asked in disbelief.

"You should see his sister!" Temutai said.

"Okay, so I guess we should match him up with . . . ," Po began, but all the other kids fled in terror.

"Get that guy from the next valley!" Lam the rabbit called out. "Peng can fight him! Peng can beat him!"

He pointed to a young leopard pushing a merchant's cart. Everyone looked at him.

"No, Lam," the young leopard said.

Jing Mei jumped off the platform.

"*Yaaa!*" He swatted at Peng's cart, knocking it over!

"Well, if you put it that way, okay," Peng said calmly.

Peng and Jing Mei climbed onto the stage and faced each other.

"Are you sure about this?" Po asked Peng.

"I am, Dragon Warrior," Peng replied.

"Okay, good luck then," Po said. That kid was gonna need it! "Fighters . . . begin!"

Jing Mei charged across the stage and started aiming punches at Peng. Peng took hold of Jing Mei's hand. He used the huge water buffalo's own force against him, easily tossing him across the stage.

"Ooooh," the crowd gasped.

Jing Mei got back on his feet, and Peng moved quickly, tossing him across the stage again. Angry, Jing Mei got up and charged Peng. Peng hit him with a series of quick, spinning kicks.

Jing Mei went down—and this time, he stayed down.

"The winner is Peng!" Po announced.

Temutai glared at his nephew. "I knew I should have brought your sister!" he growled.

"He's amazing!" Po said. Then he noticed Peng trying to slip away. "Hold on there, genius! That was some awesome kung fu. Where did you train?"

"Nowhere," Peng replied. "I have no formal training, except in pottery."

Po couldn't believe it. "You totally have to train with us at the Jade Palace!"

Temutai stomped up. "Nonsense! A warrior such as this needs to train with us in the Qidan!"

"Peng here needs to learn to do things the right way . . . at the Jade Palace," Po said.

"Sure, if he wants to be a do-nothing who postures and poses," scorned Temutai.

"Do-nothing! I'll show you nothing!" Po yelled, poking Temutai's belly.

The villagers gasped.

"You dare to poke the Warrior King of the Qidan with your finger!" Temutai fumed. "You have challenged me! For this you will pay!"

CHAPTER THREE

Temutai and Po struck battle-ready poses. Master Shifu quickly pulled Po away.

"Gentlemen, please! This is the Peace Jubilee!" Shifu reminded them.

Po and Temutai sheepishly looked at each other.

"Sorry. Our bad." Po and Temutai apologized to the crowd.

Peng stepped between them. "Please, I am not worthy to be fought over!" he pleaded. "But if I have to choose one, I choose to train at the Jade Palace!"

The villagers from the Valley of Peace all cheered. The visiting water buffalo did not look happy.

"I will be in my tent!" Temutai roared, and he stomped away.

Since there was a break in the festival, Po brought Peng up to the Jade Palace.

"And this is where the magic happens," Po said, throwing open the doors to the training room.

Inside, the Furious Five were making their way through the mechanical obstacle course. When they saw Po and Peng, they all leaped off the course to greet them.

"Nice job today, kid," Tigress told Peng. "Wanna take the Training Hall for a spin?"

"Easy, sport," Po warned him. "It's a wee bit tougher than it looks."

"*Aaaaaaiiiiieeeee!*" With a battle cry, Peng jumped right in. He destroyed spiked weapons with some hard kicks. He defended himself against spinning fighting dummies. Then he jumped in front of Po and the Furious Five and bowed respectfully. They stared at him in awe.

"Excellent job," Tigress praised him.

"Kid, you've got a future!" added Monkey.

Po suddenly felt very grumpy. He headed for his favorite spot, underneath a cherry-blossom tree on top of a mountain peak. As he munched on peaches, he thought about what he was feeling.

Peng was good—really good. A lot better than Po had been when he first came to the Jade Palace. Was the kid going to replace him? Nah, that was a silly idea, right?

Suddenly, he realized it was dark. He had to get

to the Jubilee Feast! Po hurried down the mountain.

"Without my sparkling Dragon Warrior banter, these feasts can be so boring," he mused as he walked up to the jubilee site. But as he got closer, he saw everyone laughing and having a great time. Peng was standing at the head of the table, telling stories. Everyone was laughing so hard, they didn't see Po walk up.

"Hey, what's so funny?" Po asked. "I'd like to know. Tell me."

Still, nobody noticed him.

"TELL ME!" Po yelled, a little too loudly.

That got everyone's attention. They all stared at Po.

"Uh, tell me, how are you all enjoying the feast?" Po asked.

"It's great! Grab a seat!" Monkey replied.

Po walked to his usual seat at the head of the table, where Peng was sitting.

"Sorry, Dragon Warrior. I'm in your chair," he said.

"Nonsense," Master Shifu said. "Po doesn't mind finding another seat. Do you, Po?"

"Uh, well, I guess—" Po began, but Mantis interrupted him.

"Peng! Do your Po impression again!" he yelled.

"Oh, I don't know," Peng said modestly.

"No. Really. I'd love to see it," Po said in a flat voice.

"It's really more of a tribute," Peng said. He

jumped up on top of the table and started talking in a voice like Po's. "Behold! The awesome power of the Dragon—are these dumplings?" He picked up a plate and pretended to chow down.

Everyone laughed—everyone but Po.

Maybe this new kid was going to replace him after all!

CHAPTER **FOUR**

Po couldn't sleep. He tossed and turned in his cot. Being the Dragon Warrior meant so much to him. Peng couldn't take his place, could he?

But Peng was a great fighter. And everyone liked him.

Po jumped out of bed very early in the morning. He had to talk to Master Shifu about this! Po found him outside.

"Oh, Po, there you are," Shifu said. "I've been thinking about what you said."

"You mean no-pants Fridays?" Po asked.

"No, what you said about a 'fresh face.' That's why I think the closing ceremony Tai Chi should be performed by Peng."

Po felt like he had been hit by a brick.

"Peng," he said in a tiny voice.

"Then we're agreed," Shifu said. "I'll take him the crown."

"You know what? I'll give it to Peng. I mean, after all, it was my brilliant idea to bring him here, right?" Po said.

"Good," Shifu said. "Be quick. The ceremony is tonight."

Po found Peng in the palace, signing an auto-graph for Zeng.

"Hey, I've got some news from Shifu," Po said. His paw touched the crown on his head. He knew what he was supposed to do.

But he just couldn't do it.

"Is something wrong?" Peng asked.

"Yeah, yeah. Well, no. Um, it's Shifu," Po said. "Yeah, you're just not making the cut and he, not me, thinks it would be better if you just left."

Peng looked hurt—and then his expression grew angry.

"I can't believe it. You invited me here, and now you say I'm not good enough?" he asked. His yellow eyes blazed with anger. "I'll prove to Shifu that's he's wrong! He's wrong!"

"Wait! No, Peng!" Po cried.

"You'll see!" Peng replied, and then he ran away.

Master Shifu appeared behind Po. "Where's Peng?"

Po stammered. "He, um, said no, thanks. Can you believe it? He admitted he was just using us to get famous, so he left."

Master Shifu stroked his whiskers thoughtfully. "Using us? Hmm . . . I guess it was too much to ask him to be so skilled and to be honest and pure of heart, too. Like you, Dragon Warrior."

Shifu walked off, but his words stayed with Po. He hadn't been honest and pure of heart. He had been awful.

"I gotta find Peng!" Po cried.

Peng knew exactly where he was going. He boldly strode into Temutai's tent.

"What are you doing here?" Temutai asked.

"They threw me out of the Jade Palace," Peng said angrily. "They think I'm not strong enough, and I'm here to show them they're wrong."

"Ha! Yes! By training with me!" Temutai said triumphantly.

"No," Peng said. He grabbed a sword and pointed it at the warrior. "By showing them that I can destroy you!"

Temutai's eyes grew wide. "That's different!"

CHAPTER FIVE

Peng lunged at Temutai, swinging the sword. Temutai picked up a table to shield himself from the blows. Then he pushed forward, sending Peng flying.

But Peng was determined. He attacked again.

"Ha!" Peng cried. He swung the sword again— and Po's paw grabbed it. He stood between Temutai and the blow.

"You are defending me?" asked a puzzled Temutai.

"Yeah. Weird, huh?" Po replied.

"Out of my way so I can finish him!" Peng demanded. He swung the sword again. Po quickly grabbed a small stool to defend himself.

"Peng! Stop!" he cried.

"I've practiced my kung fu with no plans, no dreams, until you gave me one—and then Shifu snatched it away!" Peng cried.

He charged at Po, pushing him backward into Temutai. The two oversize warriors crashed to the floor.

"Are you okay?" Po asked.

"No, I am not, and it is your fault!" Temutai yelled, jumping to his feet. Po, Temutai, and Peng stood in a triangle. Nobody was exactly sure who was fighting whom. So they all started fighting one another!

The fight spilled into the village—and right into the closing ceremony of the Peace Jubilee!

Po tossed a wagon at Temutai. Peng kicked Po, sending him flying back into a food cart. The food cart knocked into Mrs. Yoon, who banged into the pig behind her. Angry, the pig shoved her, and she shoved him back. Soon, everyone in the village was fighting!

The Furious Five jumped into the action to help Po, but Temutai's water-buffalo guards stood in their way. Now they were fighting too.

Po looked around. This was terrible, and it was all his fault!

"Stop it!" he yelled as loudly as he could.

Everyone froze.

Po looked at Peng. "Peng, you don't understand!"

"Understand what?" Peng asked.

"I lied, Peng," admitted Po. "Shifu didn't want you gone. I did. It's just, like, all of a sudden everyone was digging you, and I was all jealous and mad and I wanted to wear this stupid crown. Peng, I'm sorry."

Po tossed the crown onto the ground.

"And so am I," Peng said. He picked up the crown and handed it to Po. "I apologize for my anger, Dragon Warrior."

Po put the crown back on and grinned. Temutai smiled down at him. "I like the jaunty angle!"

Po laughed. "Let's get this jubilee on the road!"

It was time for the ceremonial Tai Chi. Po, Temutai, and Peng did it together. Po felt happy and at peace. After all, he was, and always would be, the Dragon Warrior!